Simon Spotlight
New York London Toronto Sydney

Based on the television series *Rubbadubbers*™ created by HIT Entertainment PLC, as seen on Nick Jr.®

adapted by Lauryn Silverhardt
based on a book by Jackie Andrews
photos by HOT Animation

SIMON SPOTLIGHT
An imprint of Simon & Schuster Children's Publishing Division
1230 Avenue of the Americas, New York, New York 10020

Manufactured in the United States of America
First Edition
2 4 6 8 10 9 7 5 3 1
ISBN 0-689-86547-3

Laughter and noisy splashes filled the bathroom. The Rubbadubbers were playing soccer in the bath!

"We're winning!" yelled Sploshy. "Splish! Splash! Splosh!"

"Hey, watch this!" cried Tubb. "Oops!"

The ball flew up and bounced off Reg's head.

“Thanks, Reg!” called Tubb. “Good thing you were keeping guard, or we would have lost the ball!”

“Well, it’s all I’m good for,” grumbled Reg. “I can’t go in the water. I’d get rusty.”

Reg tossed the ball back to Tubb.

"I'm tired of being a ball guard," Reg said to himself. "*If only* I could go under water—I could have some fun too!"

Suddenly . . .

Reg found himself under water.
"Wow!" exclaimed Reg. "I'm swimming! And I'm *not* rusting!"

He swam off to explore, and he found Tubb and Sploshy in a beautiful underwater palace.

"We're the king and queen," said Tubb.

"We're glad you've arrived because we've been guarding this treasure for ages!" cried Sploshy.

"Our last underwater robot was eaten by a monster!" said Sploshy.

"But now that you're here," said Tubb, "we can go out again. Just don't let the monster in!"

"What does the monster look like?" asked Reg.

"Well, he's got *big* teeth and *big* eyes," said Tubb.

"And he does *not* have a moustache!" added Sploshy as they swam away.

Reg went over to the treasure and stood guard.

While standing guard, Reg heard a knock on the palace door.

“It’s the treasure checker,”
said a familiar voice.

"I wonder if this is the monster," Reg said to himself. "He's got *big* teeth and *big* eyes. But he's got a moustache! That's all right, then! Come in!"

"I've come to check if your treasure needs fixing," said Finbar.

"Oh, right," said Reg. "Go ahead."

Finbar looked at the treasure.

"Well, what do you know!" he cried. "It's broken!"

“Are you going to fix it?” asked Reg.
“Oh, yes,” said Finbar. “But I don’t have all the parts here. I’ll have to take it away with me.”

So Finbar picked up the treasure and swam away with it.

Finbar chuckled. "Argh, argh! The mighty monster strikes again!"

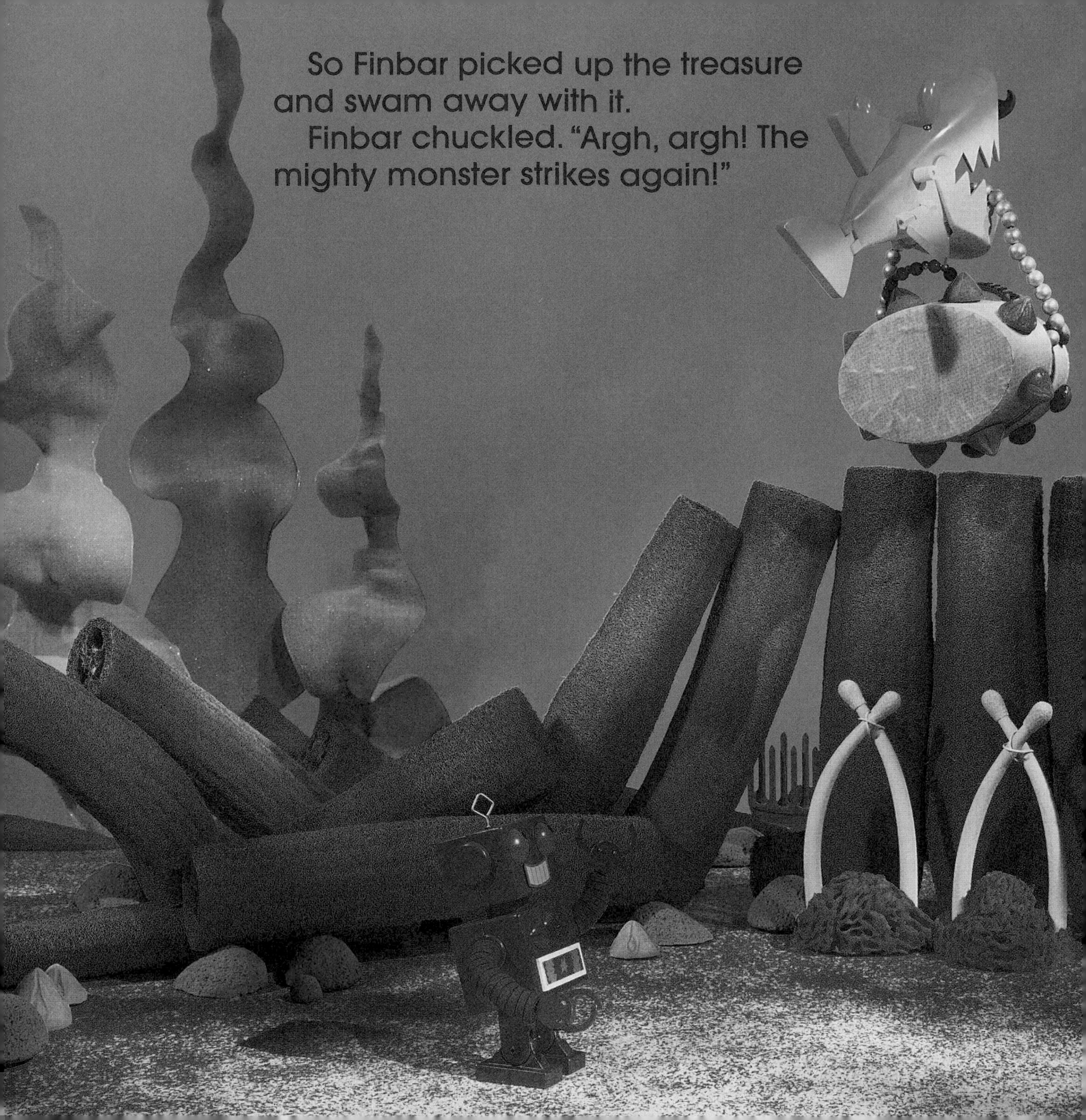

Unfortunately Finbar's false moustache came unglued.

"Oh, no!" said Reg. "He does *not* have a moustache! It's the monster!"

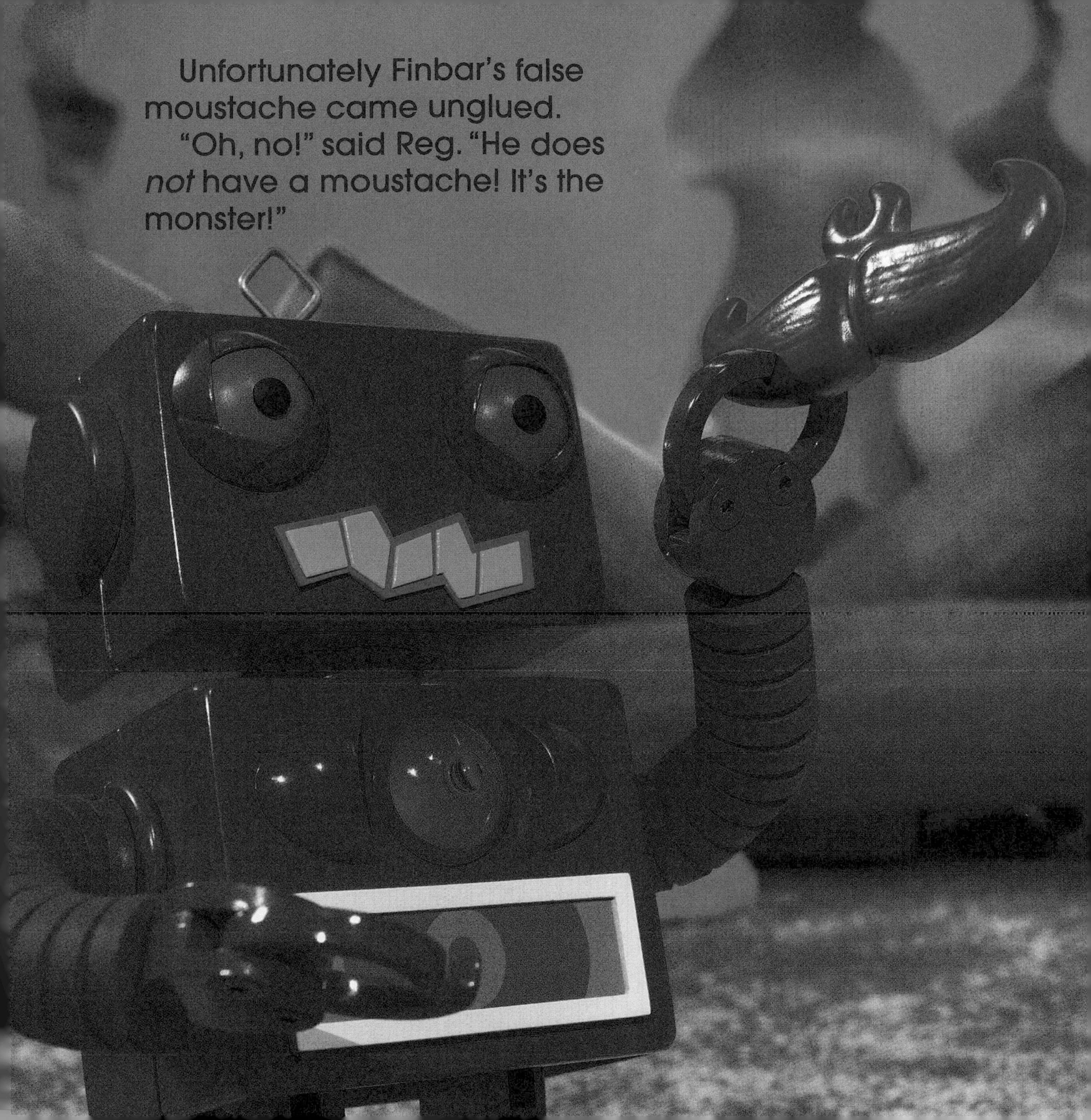

Reg swam after Finbar, but his arms got tired.

"I'm a useless underwater robot!" said Reg.

Then Reg had an idea. Maybe if he blew a big bubble, he could float inside it, instead of swimming. Reg blew the bubble and steered it so he soon caught up with Finbar.

At that moment his bubble burst. Reg bumped into Finbar, who dropped the treasure in surprise. Reg, Finbar, and the treasure fell through the water . . .

. . . all the way down to the palace, where Tubb and Sploshy were staring at the empty space where their treasure had been.

Tubb and Sploshy gave Reg a reward, and they asked him to guard their treasure forever.

But Reg didn't like underwater life. "Why don't you ask the monster?" he said. "If he's guarding it, he won't steal it!"

"Do you want the job?" asked Tubb.

"It'd be fin-tastic!" said Finbar.

"Now, *if only* I could get back on dry land. . . ." said Reg.

And then . . .

Reg was back home, standing by the bathtub.

"Ah, this is better!" he said. The other Rubbadubbers were still playing soccer.

"Hey, Reg!" called Tubb, as the ball flew out again. "Send our ball back, will you?"

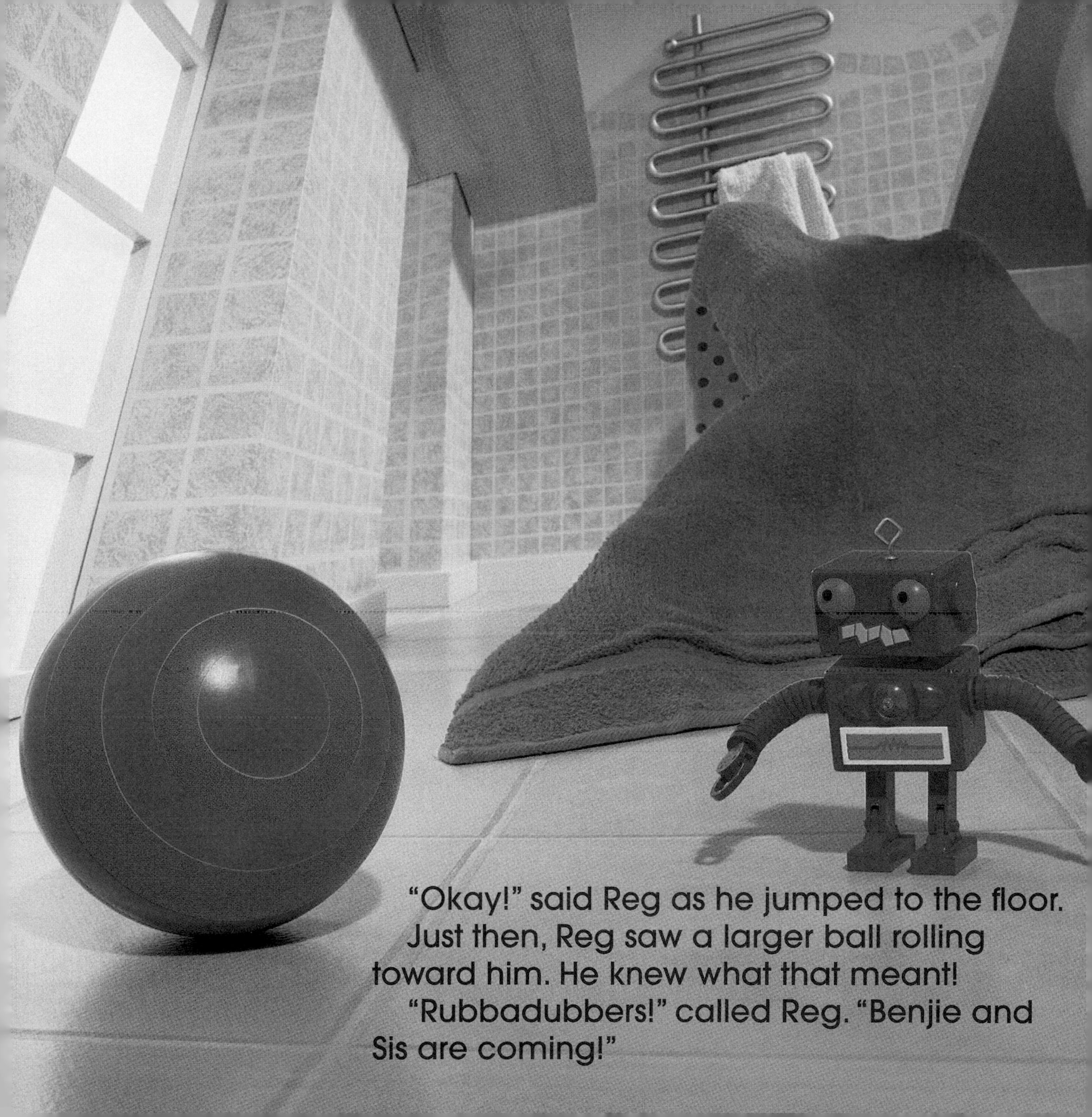

"Okay!" said Reg as he jumped to the floor.

Just then, Reg saw a larger ball rolling toward him. He knew what that meant!

"Rubbadubbers!" called Reg. "Benjie and Sis are coming!"

"It's bathtime, Rubbadubbers!" cried Tubb. "Swimmin'!" And he dove into the water.